# No More Pencils, No More Books, No More Teacher's Dirty Looks!

## Diane deGroat

SCHOLASTIC INC.

New York  Toronto  London  Auckland  Sydney
Mexico City  New Delhi  Hong Kong  Buenos Aires

ISBN-13: 978-0-439-02005-3
ISBN-10: 0-439-02005-0

12 11 10 9 8 7 6 5 4 3                                                                      7 8 9 10 11 12/0

Printed in the U.S.A.                                                                       40

First Scholastic printing, May 2007

Typography by Jeanne L. Hogle

"Hooray," Gilbert shouted, heading for the door. "Today's the last day of school!"

"Here are the cookies," Mother said. "And your present for Mrs. Byrd." She put the cookies and the present into his backpack.

As he ran out the door, Gilbert waved and said, "Don't forget to come to the party this afternoon. Mrs. Byrd is giving out awards!"

Patty was waiting for him outside. She looked sad. "I'm going to miss school," she said. "I like being in Mrs. Byrd's class."

"Me too," Gilbert said. "But I like summer vacation better."

When they got to the classroom, Mrs. Byrd was changing the number on the countdown banner. Yesterday it said, 2 DAYS OF SCHOOL LEFT! Today it said, 1 DAY OF SCHOOL LEFT! Mrs. Byrd didn't look very sad.

Lewis ran into the classroom, singing, "No more pencils, no more books, no more teacher's dirty looks. . . ."

Mrs. Byrd heard him, but she didn't give him a dirty look. She just smiled and said, "Settle down, everyone. We have a lot to do this morning, starting with cleaning out our desks."

"My desk is already clean," Philip said proudly.

Lewis rolled his eyes and said, "Maybe you'll get the 'clean desk' award."

"No," Philip said back. "I'm going to get the 'best reader' award. Everyone knows I'm the best reader in the class."

Gilbert wondered if he would get an award. He wasn't the best reader, and he certainly didn't have the cleanest desk!

Neither did Mrs. Byrd. When she emptied out her bottom drawer, four big packs of gum spilled onto the floor. "Oh, my!" she said. "Here is your gum, Lewis. You can have it back now."

"That's okay," Lewis answered, scraping the green paint off the side of his desk. "You can keep it to remember me by."

Mrs. Byrd laughed and said, "I don't think I could ever forget you, Lewis!"

Before lunch they practiced their songs and poems for the parents. Frank was nervous, and Mrs. Byrd told him to pretend that everyone in the audience was sitting in their underwear. That made Frank giggle, and he wasn't nervous anymore.

"Thanks," Frank said. "My grandma and grandpa are coming, and I don't want to mess up." Then he giggled at the thought of his grandparents sitting in the audience in their underwear!

"You will all do fine," Mrs. Byrd said proudly when they were finished. "And remember: After the poems I'll give out the awards, so remain seated at the front of the room."

At recess Gilbert and Patty talked about who might get awards. "Philip is the best reader, for sure," Gilbert said.

"Frank is good in math," Patty added. "He might get a math award."

"And you're the best speller, Patty," said Gilbert. "I know you'll get an award for that."

Patty smiled and said, "Well, you're the best at . . . at . . ."

Before she could think of what Gilbert did best, Lewis said,
"What's the big deal? Everybody gets an award."

Gilbert hoped that was true, but he didn't know what he
was the best at!

When they returned to the classroom, all the desks were clean. All the books were boxed. And all the supplies were packed. It didn't feel like Mrs. Byrd's classroom anymore. Just as Gilbert started to feel sad, the parents began to arrive.

Then Gilbert started to feel nervous. He said his
poem over and over in his head.

Mrs. Byrd welcomed everyone. Then her class sang
the songs they had practiced. Lewis sang the loudest,
and Gilbert wondered if there was
a "loud singer" award!

Soon it was time for Gilbert to recite the first poem. He took a deep breath and stepped forward. He said, "Summer's here. I can't wait. But first grade was really great! Mrs. Byrd's the very best. Even when she gives a test!"

Gilbert sat down again. Whew! He didn't make a single mistake. Maybe he would get an award for the best poem!

But Margaret's was good also: "We learned to spell. We learned to read. We learned a lot of things indeed!"

Even Frank said his poem without a single mistake: "I love numbers, I love math. I think of counting, even in the bath."

But when it was Philip's turn to recite the last poem, he didn't step forward. His knees were wobbly, and he looked very pale. He had forgotten his poem!

Mrs. Byrd handed him a copy, but when Philip tried to read it, all that came out was a squeak.

Gilbert's little sister, Lola, started to laugh, and Gilbert gave her a dirty look. No one knew what to do, so Gilbert took the paper and started reading: "Each day in school . . . I try to be . . . as good a student as I can be. And if I have one book, or three—"

Then Philip finally remembered the rest, and blurted out, "I'll always have a friend with me!"

Everyone clapped, and Philip turned red.

Philip was still red when Mrs. Byrd gave him the "best reader" award. Patty got the spelling award, Margaret got one for handwriting, and Kenny had the best attendance. Even Lewis got an award for being the funniest.

Gilbert stood there as, one by one, the ribbons were given out. He thought he might get the "best artist" award, but Susan got it instead. Maybe there wouldn't be an award for Gilbert after all!

Finally Mrs. Byrd said, "And the last award goes to Gilbert. He gets the 'good friend' award."

Gilbert was happy. Now he knew what he was good at! He thought Mrs. Byrd was the best teacher ever.

As they ate cookies and cake, Mrs. Byrd said, "I have a gift for each of you to take home—a memory book of pictures from your first-grade class."

"Hey," Lewis said, flipping through the pages. "Here's the snowman that Gilbert helped me make."

"And our trip to Pilgrim Town!" Philip added. "Gilbert was my buddy on the bus."

On the last page of the memory book was a picture of the whole class, including Mrs. Byrd. "I'm really going to miss you all," she said. She looked like she was going to cry.

Good Luck in Grade 2

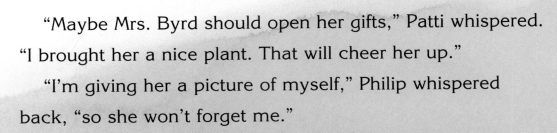

"Maybe Mrs. Byrd should open her gifts," Patti whispered. "I brought her a nice plant. That will cheer her up."

"I'm giving her a picture of myself," Philip whispered back, "so she won't forget me."

Gilbert's gift was a T-shirt that said, "#1 Teacher." Now he wished that he was giving her a picture of himself. What if she forgot who Gilbert was!

Sadly, Gilbert said to Mrs. Byrd, "I wish you could always be our teacher."

Mrs. Byrd smiled and said, "Me too. But remember— you can still visit me when you're in second grade."

"It's not the same," Gilbert answered quietly.

The bell rang, and everyone took turns hugging Mrs. Byrd, until Mrs. Byrd was all hugged out.

As they walked home, Gilbert said, "Mrs. Byrd looked so sad when we left. What will she do all summer without us?"

Patty sighed and said, "She'll probably be busy getting ready for her new class."

Then Gilbert started to sniffle. "Mrs. Byrd was awfully, awfully sad," he said. "She's going to miss me very, very much!"

"Hmmm," Father said. "I know what will make you feel better." They were standing in front of the ice-cream shop.

Gilbert saw all of his friends inside, and he
started to feel better. No one looked sad at all.
Everyone was happy that summer vacation
was finally here.

Especially Mrs. Byrd!